Clint Faraday
#20
Dead Ahead

Clint and Judi are driving home from a visit with friends and are approaching Hornitos when Judi remarks that there's a fire dead ahead. They stop to help. It is a burning house. When Clint goes inside there is a body on the bed. A body that died from a broken neck, not a fire.

Contents

About the author

CD Moulton has traveled extensively over much of the world both in the music business, where he was a rock guitarist, songwriter and arranger and in an import/export business. He has been everything from a bar owner to auto salvage (junkyard) manager, longshoreman to high steel worker, orchid grower to landscaper, tropical fish farmer to commercial fisherman. He started writing books in 1983 and has published more than 350 books as of January 1, 2023. His most popular books to date are about research with orchids, though much of his science fiction and fantasy work has proven popular. He wrote the CD Grimes, PI series, and the Det. Nick Storie series, Clint Faraday series, and many other works.

He now resides in Gualaca, Chiriqui, Panamá, where he writes books, plays music with friends, does research with orchids and medicinal plants. He has lately become involved in fighting for the rights of the indigenous people, who are among his closest friends, and in fighting the extreme corruption in the courts and police in Panamá.

He offers the free e-book, *Fading Paradise*, that explains what he has been through because of the corruption.

CD is the discoverer of the Chadam Protocol for curing cancer.

Facebook page Ambrosia peruviana for cancer.

Clint Faraday #20
Dead Ahead

<u>*Prologue*</u>

Clint Faraday sighed and looked at his wrist-watch. 3:35. Two more hours to Chiriqui Grande. They'd spend the night with friends there. He and his attractive nextdoor neighbor in Bocas Town, Isla Colón, Bocas del Toro, Panamá, Judi Lum, a smart oriental woman who was as much as a partner in his detective cases anymore, were returning to Bocas after spending the past two days in Rio Sereno and Volcan, visiting friends. It was a good time, but was exhausting. They had climbed two mountains on foot in two days. They had a box of orchids they found where some Indios were cutting timber for building a house. They, like their mentor and friend, Dave, would never take the plants unless they were doomed where they were. Dave was a nutty musician/ botanist who was accepted by the Indios, as was Judi, though not to the point Clint was. Clint had been declared a Ngobe by two of the chiefs of the comarca, an honor he was only the second person to be given, as they understood it.

Dave would care for the plants that were new or different from what he had. Clint and Judi would take the rest home, along with Ben and Earl, two neighbors/friends in Bocas.

Clint had sworn to never again own a car when he moved from Florida to Panamá, but events had as much as forced him to buy one. It did come in handy for these trips, he had to admit, but he would prefer taking the buses that are everywhere and very cheap in Panamá.

"Want me to drive?" Judi asked. "You look like you could use a rest."

He agreedm and stopped to exchange seats. Judi was actually a better driver than he. She knew the road.

They chatted a little as they proceeded. They stopped in Gualaca to say "Hello!" to people they knew, and to have a melacatón (peach nectar) and use the baños. After about fifteen minutes, they proceeded on upward into the mountains and were nearing Hornitos when Judi said, "There seems to be a fire, dead ahead. It's bigger than a weed burn. I hope it's not someone's house, up here. By the time a fire truck could get here there wouldn't be anything but ashes."

They came to the fire, a small house, indeed. Several people were carrying buckets of water to dump on it. The house was gutted, but the walls were concrete and the roof was zinc-plated steel. Clint offered his help, and Judi went to help the women filling the pails. The fire was mostly out when a man came out and said that Pablo Quintero was inside, dead. He must have fallen asleep in the bed and left the stove on or something. It was bad! He looked scared more than upset.

Clint looked around the house and shook his head, then went in to find a badly burned body laying on some sooty smoldering bedsprings. He looked at the body, mostly just bones, and shook his head again. "His neck was broken. He didn't die in any fire!"

"Dios mio!" the man cried.

<u>*Chapter one*</u>

"Anthony Garcia, called Tonio by the people around here. You are the famous Clint Faraday and the knockout secretary who keeps him from drinking too much and gives excuses for his being a total violence freak asshole, Judi?" the police investigator said, in perfect English, when he was presented to Clint and Judi. "I'm friends with Sergio Sanchez. Work with him on rotation, sometimes."

"Well, he's the *in*famous PI ,and I'm his sexy moll secretary who actually runs the agency, so maybe that's about right. So. What's it to you, Flatfoot?" Judi said, with a laugh.

"You read too much crap from the states," Clint said. "Any idea what this is about?"

"I don't read much. I do watch TV.

"I don't know. Pablo was fairly well-liked. He never caused any trouble. I'll have to dig things up. You saw that it was murder when you came into the room, according to Santos Riveras. I can see what you saw, I think. His head was twisted almost backward. I'd say his killer was pretty big."

"A karate move. He was strong, but maybe not big," Clint said. "You've undoubtably seen that twist bit on TV. Headlock from behind with one arm, wrap around the head with the other and twist, while shoving the body forward. Fast."

Tonio nodded. "I thought that was fake, but maybe it works. I've seen wrestlers do it, and it didn't seem to hurt anybody for more than a few seconds."

"It's dangerous. They have to practice enough that they won't overdo it and manage to actually break somebody's neck."

"Oh, come on! Everybody knows that stuff's real! They don't actually *practice* anything, do they?"

Clint gave him the old bird. They checked around the house together. Clint was known to the police in Panamá as someone who would work with them and wouldn't try to hog credit for what they did. Mostly the opposite, he would see they got the credit for most of what he did, whenever possible.

"Okay. The way I see it, he met someone and they got into some kind of argument. It got out of hand, and somebody who saw that move on TV tried it. It worked. He panicked and set the fire to make it look like a housefire accident," Tonio suggested. "Close to what you saw?"

Clint thought, and shook his head. "It takes too much force. Whoever did that meant to kill. The maneuver takes a lot of practice or all you'll do is sprain the neck muscles and give someone a mean headache and sore neck for a few days. If it was an accident, the person who did it still had a lot of practice, and would know he was killing the subject. It's a violent twist that has to happen before the neck muscles contract and the guy gets up and kicks hell out of you. There's something either professional or very emotional behind it. I think, if it was professional, there would be a reason we can find behind it. If it wasn't, the person who did it will have been noted as having some kind of argument with him. Either way, we should be able to find this one."

"I'm glad of one thing," Tonio said. "You keep saying 'we' – so I can expect your help on this? It's not the kind of thing we have here – I mean this area. I know you've had experience among the gringos and in Panamá City. It's way beyond my own training or experience."

"He was an Indio. I'm a Ngobe."

"I heard about that. Clements said the governor in Bocas was livid about it. The way they treat some of the indigenos there makes them scared shitless you'll go after them."

"All they have to do is give everyone an even

break. No more problem."

"They do. They screw everyone they can. The problem is, that includes the indigenos." He laughed.

"So? Give the Indios special treatment by *not* trying to screw them every chance they get. I might even approve of that!"

"Much too deep for their limited intelligence. It wouldn't occur to them."

Clint grinned, noddedm and replied. "Well, all seriousness aside, we should solve this in a few minutes."

Tonio looked like he wanted to say something, thought, and said, "I think I like you. You said the exact truth of the matterm then!"

They went outsidem where Judi was talking with several of the women. She looked at Clint and shrugged very slightly. She hadn't learned anything yet – and she was as expert at getting information innocently as anyone he ever knew. It could be because they didn't know anything, or it could be self-protection. They didn't dare say what they knew or they might die in a fire. If it was that, Clint would know very quickly. They wouldn't say anything past a certain point that gossip always passed from the get-go.

The next step was the obvious. Tonio would handle most of it. Clint would go on to Bocas, where Judi would go on to Bocas Town with the groceries, orchids, and stuff. He'd be able to get back early in the morning. He wanted to check on a few things later today and in Chiriqui Grande tonight.

The rest of the way to Bocas wasn't so bad. He picked up two Indio friends, Milo and Betany, at the Norteño bus stop casita, and took them to the hospital in Almirante. Betany was having the baby, any minute. Clint was afraid he'd end up having to deliver it before they got there, but they made it with almost forty minutes to go. The bus they would have taken would have given them just enough time if they got a taxi at the station. This was Betany's first, but she'd seen dozens of births before, and wasn't much concerned. Milo wasn't worrued, either. The Indios took such normal things in stride. They lived with nature.

Clint was able to learn that Pablo had come to Chiriqui Grande regularly. He had a girlfriend who worked in the aduana. They were planning to get married whenever she became pregnant. He got along with everyone fairly well, though he seemed to have some kind of issue with some people who came from Colombia. They were only there about once in two months. No one knew what it was about, but Pablo always warned people not to trust them. It could have been because most people were already suspicious of Colombians.

It didn't seem like much. Clint had learned, long ago, that what seemed like nothing was far too often the most important part of a case.

He dropped Judi off at the place in Almirante where he kept his boat when going anywhere from that part of the mainland. Judi was expert with the boat. She would have no trouble, though it was a bit windy, and would be rough. She took that in stride like the Indios took things in stride. He said he didn't know when he'd be back. Probably not long. He'd stay in Chiriqui Grande for the night to see what he could learn. He had found one connection he wanted to investigate, already.

Brian was on the dock for the water taxi, so Judi would take him and his stuff to Bocas Town. Clint headed back for Chiriqui Grande, getting there just after dark. He checked into the hotel and went for dinner at a new little restaurant he had never heard of. He wished he hadn't heard of it when he left. The food was blah and expensive, and the waitress had an attitude. She seemed to think anyone should be honored that she would condescend to wait on them. He was glad of the Panamanian custom of not tipping. This was the first one he'd been in anywhere in Panamá where the service was so bad he wouldn't have left a tip.

Next was the local gathering place for the Indios, a small bar. It was noisy and fun, and he learned what he wanted to learn about Pablo and the people around. He also learned what might be the reason for the service at the little restaurant. It was a place a gringo bought and set up for Linda – his girlfriend. He had plenty of money, but wasn't going to support any woman who wouldn't do anything for herself. He didn't come into Chiriqui Grande more than once a week, and didn't know the restaurant wasn't popular. If you wanted a pretty good meal there, along with good service, make it on Saturday night or during the day Sunday, when he was there. Everyone knew it, and would eat there when he was in town.

"He doesn't catch on to why the place doesn't make a profit?" Clint asked Emilio, a friend who was up on all the happenings around the area.

"He doesn't know it. It's up to her to take care of everything. He just gives her money to buy new equipment or tables and dishes or whatever. She rips him off for most of that stuff, and makes enough on the two days to get by. I think she deliberately runs the people away because she doesn't like to have to cook or to do anything. I thought you had sense enough not to go into any restaurant that had no customers at dinnertime!"

"There were some few backpackers and surfers there. I did notice they only had sodas."

"She has them come in. They get a soda and read the menu, look at the prices, and leave."

Clint shook his head and grimaced. "Why don't any of you tell the gringo idiot what's going on?"

"We don't like him."

"Oh? Arrogant asshole?"

"Not really too bad. He's just the type who won't even say 'Buenos!' unless you do first. He's just not ... he's like too many gringos, but mostly the ones up around Boquete. Always talking about money and stocks and such. Nobody here cares about any fucking stock market!"

"Got money, or talks about it?"

"I suppose he's got plenty. He wastes a lot."

Clint talked awhile, then went back to the hotel. Something was way out of sync, here! It didn't have anything to do with his case. This was a type of thing there was too much of around. That running customers away was a big part of it. Him coming into town and she acting 180 degrees different gave it away. No one could actually be that stupid. The books would probably show the place was taking in thousands of dollars a day. It was money laundering. Probably not a lot, unless he had several such places. Linda was the one who was stupid. She didn't realize she was set up to take the fall if they were caught. All he would know was that he helped her now and then with minor funds, and took her word for it that the place was barely making a living for her. *She* was the one who kept the books! He would be shocked and enraged that he was so used!

Clint was about to fall asleep when something else occurred to him. Maybe there was a direct connection. It would depend on whether certain people were in town at the same time just a bit too often.

What had Pablo stumbled on that got him killed?

<u>*Chapter two*</u>

In the morning he talked with Julio and Berto, two Indio friends, about Pablo, Linda, George Blanton (Linda's boyfriend), and the Colombians, Simon and Pancho Vallardes and Donaldo Perez. The Colombians had been in Chiriqui Grande about a week ago, but had driven back toward Panamá City. They had a dark red Mitsubishi truck with lots of fancy chrome. Everyone was more or less neutral about them. They weren't liked, but they weren't *dis*liked either. They didn't mix with the locals much, and everyone liked it that way. They were sort of up-end average size, and strong. They looked like family, but who knew? The brothers wore too much flashy jewelry, and the other one smoked cigars.

Clint had his car, so drove on to La Mina. The Colombians weren't noted as being there, though there was a man who talked like a Colombian who hung around a couple of days. He came from David and went back at night, then came back the following day and was around the China and the carretera, then went back to David or somewhere the second day, about four thirty or so. A week ago, yesterday. Nobody heard him called anything, and the police at the toll station hadn't spoken with him at all. He was about five nine or ten and maybe a hundred eighty five or ninety pounds, had thick black hair and fairly sharp features. There was a small part of his left ear missing – like someone bit a piece off in a fight, or something.

"Did he smoke?" Clint asked. Everyone looked at each other. Most of them shrugged. Virginia, a waitress, said he carried a couple of cigars in his shirt pocket, but she didn't ever see him smoking them. He wanted mariscos, but they didn't have anything fresh when he was there. He did say something about a good restaurant in David with a seven in the name, or maybe it was Caribe. Maybe both.

Clint thanked them, and left. He would go to David. The man had come on the bus, both times, and left on it, both times. There was a restaurant that was known to serve very good seafood just past the airport, Mar Caribe, and there was a place called Siete Mares (seven seas) not far from Cervantes Park. La Tipica was another good bet for good seafood. Clint was fairly certain the man who was noted hanging around La Mina would prove to be Donaldo Perez. He had hung around

La Mina because Pablo was from the area. Pablo had come to town and been followed to his place. Perez or the Vallartes would be the killer.

Now to discover what the killing and fire was about. Money laundering, almost certainly, but Clint didn't think it was drug money because of the way the Colombians were acting. The drug people usually would let it be known they were "connected" and would try to intimidate people, though that wasn't nearly as strong a trait as it sounded. These were too quiet, and didn't use the normal tactics. It was just a feeling. It didn't *feel* like a drug connection.

Clint checked into the Hotel Iris, considered using a disguise, and rejected it. They wouldn't know he was interested in them. The people he'd talked with was just in a conversational way, and they didn't know any of them, anyhow. He went to Peter's for a good meal, Jimmy the German had taken over the restaurant, and his weiner schnitzel was already much talked about, but he had soon given up the restaurant. The atmosphere wasn't right, and he couldn't make a living there.

He talked with a few regulars, Wilson and Tina and Harry were there, from Bocas, Larry had been in the hospital, but was alright. John and Rick were at their accustomed spot on the balcony, talking with Corky. Alan and Walt were going to Sandy's, CD was talking with Rita and a gringo from Boquete, Jessy was mixing rum and cokes – all typical. It was like he'd been there last night.

He decided to go to the Seven Seas for some mariscos. Everyone said there was a new owner at the little bar in front of the restaurant who played a lot of gringo music and spoke excellent English, though that wasn't important to Clint. He could use a difference in the music.

He immediately met Ulyses, the bar owner, and they discussed music and whatever else came up. Ulyses knew Dave, Clint's nutty musician/botanist friend. He didn't remember seeing the Colombians, which meant nothing. He didn't see a lot of the restaurant customers, and he wouldn't have noticed them much if they were at the bar, but outside. They were ordinary types. Soon Walt and Alan and their dates/girlfriends came in, they chatted a few minutes, then Clint drove out to the Mare Caribe to have a great corvina dinner. He was leaving when a dark red Mitsubishi truck with lots of chrome and three men in it drove in. It would be too suspicious if he went back now, so he drove across into Pedrigal, around behind some large hibiscus plants where he waited for them to leave. When they did leave, an hour and a half later, they went directly to La Esmeralda, a semi-famous brothel. He wasn't about to wait to follow them later, so went back to his hotel. He wouldn't have much trouble finding them. That over-chromed truck would be easy to trace. Unless they had a place in or near, David they would be in an expensive hotel. Ask the attendant if the truck was on the hotel lot.

The Best Western and the Ciudad de David were the top picks. He checked, and found they weren't staying at either. Next, the Alcalá, then Iberia and a few others, but they weren't in any of the downtown hotels. He checked the ones on the main carretera, where an Indio friend working in a car wash said they were staying at a place near the Rey Mall. A friend or something. The truck was parked in the garage a lot of the time.

Clint checked the registro publica to find the place was owned by a Raul Aparicio R. Aparicio lived in Penonomé and leased the place to a small company in Santa Marta, Colombia. Luz Futura Inversiones. A check with his friend, Manolo, an undercover agent for Interpol *et al,* told him the company wasn't even mildly suspected of having connections with the drug trade, which was a relief. Manolo said they had a Russian partner in the company, as well as two Israelis, French, and Spanish.

Next, the modern way to learn about almost anything: computer. The net showed the company invested in jewelry, art, precious metals, and whatever came along that was both portable and expensive, preferably those things that would appreciate a lot for collectors' value.

Manolo didn't know anything about that kind of company? Interpol?

He called Manolo back. "What's the skinny? For real this time? Not some line where Interpol isn't interested in a company that deals in the very things Interpol was established for."

"Clint, I honestly don't have any information. Let me check internal and I'll get back."

They chatted a minute or two, then Clint went to a steak dinner at Las Brasas. Rib-eye that was excellent. Las Brasas is known for great filets and steaks. He met Yvonne, a girl he knew in Bocas Town, and they spent a great night together.

In the morning Clint checked around to learn where the three Colombians hung around, mostly. He found them eating breakfast at La Tipica and followed them to a junkyard, then to a towing company, then to a house on the road to Dolega. Manolo called and said the company was only active in Colombia, and everything checked out about them.

"Not even maybe!" Clint protested. "Why do

they have that leased place here? Why are they going to the places where they're going? Who lives in the big brick house with the huge yard and security fences no one could get past near Anastasia? What's going on with a gringo and girlfriend working an obvious money-laundering scheme in Chiriqui Grande? Why was Pablo Quintero murdered?"

"I would maybe get a little suspicious if they're going to odd places, and a lot more if they're involved in a money-laundry. What about this Pablo person? Murder?"

"They meet with a George Blanton in Chiriqui Grande every couple of weeks. Linda, Blanton's supposed Panamanian girlfriend, has a restaurant that serves bad food with a worse attitude, unless Blanton is in town, when everything's hunky-dory. Pablo saw or knew something. He was killed with a karate move, and his place burned down around him. Perez, one of the Colombians, was hanging around in Hornitos where Pablo lived for two days, then Pablo's killed and he goes back to David to stay with Simon and Pancho Vallardes in that leased place. DUH! Chew'n gum!"

"I see. I think maybe I'll take on a little personal investigation. I'll need bait."

"Dave has a Carl Griesbaum automaton he's

been trying to sell, but no one in Panamá seems interested in those type really good antiques. They're supposedly looking for art and such. It's worth a couple of grand, but it appreciates fast for that kind of thing. There won't ever be anymore."

"Okay. It's worth a try. If he loses it without compensation Interpol will pay for it, okay?"

"As you say, it's worth a try!"

He called Dave, who was in Cusapín. "Why the hell not? Judi can get it for you. She has the keys to my place."

Now to put something together. If he could produce a reason, motive, he could close this one out fast. It could get interesting if it led to some kind of international theft scheme – or worse!

<u>*Chapter three*</u>

The somewhat stocky younger man with a mustache and cane who much resembled Clint Faraday took the box he carried into the exclusive gift shop across from Rey. He met the woman who owned the place, Lila Green, an attractive Israeli woman, and asked if she could possibly find a buyer for a special item. It seemed to him that Panamanians weren't much for collecting rare antiques.

Lila Green was the wife of Harold Green, who was the uncle of one George Blanton, who lived near Chiriqui Grande, Bocas del Toro, Panamá. Judi had given him the name and address when he told her that George Blanton was somehow involved in a money laundering scheme. She had met him and his girlfriend about five months ago in Chiriqui Grande when she was trying out a new restaurant Blanton was opening for his girlfriend.

There was nobody like Judi Lum for finding information! This one was a simple coincidence. Lila and Harold green were there for the opening. If Judi hadn't been there and Clint wanted the information, she would have found it in a day, when it would have taken him a week.

Lila shrugged and said to show it to her, and she'd possibly be able to find a buyer – for a price. He opened the package and took out the hand-carved automaton. She gasped, and cried, "It's a Griesbaum! Where did you find it? It looks perfect! The last one I saw had the lamp and mop broken – and sold for nearly two thousand dollars! It's perfect! All of Griesbaum's work is unique. It's truly one of a kind! This one is ... about nineteen nineteen or twenty. It's perfect!

"I know. You're selling it for a friend who found it in an attic when his grandmother died and whatever."

"No. It's the property of a friend in Bocas. He got it from a Dr. Averbush, in Florida, in the fifties. It's totally legitimate. It works perfectly, except the bellows – it's paper, you know – needs repair. The glue came apart."

"They all do. That's a very minor thing, and doesn't affect the value. As I said, one of these fourteen inch carvings was broken in two places and the mop part was gone. If it was a later one by someone else they would have probably used it for firewood, or something, but it's a Griesbaum.

"Bottom line."

"He wants five grand, but knows that's hopeless, here. Make an offer."

"If he can wait a year or so, the five grand would be a good deal. Now, I'll have to contact a man in Sant ... a friend in the business somewhere else. I'll have an offer this evening? Five thirty?

"It won't be for more than three. He's more a ... collector for appreciation."

"I'll be back." He rewrapped the package, saluted with the cane, and started out.

"Wait! I don't even know who you are!" she cried.

"Oh! Right. I'm James Hanrady." He went on out.

She expected it was stolen. That told Clint all he really wanted to know. They were dealing in stolen art. Manolo would need that information, so he called. He wanted to connect and prove the murder. Manolo could handle the international theft and fencing part. That's what he did.

Clint sat in his car to think for a minute. He'd solved the case, and had everything he needed, except motive. It was obvious Pablo saw or knew something dangerous to the Colombians – wasn't it? Was it necessarily them? What about Blanton and Linda? Come to think of it, what about that towing company? A junkyard, they could be looking for antiques no one knew were antiques. That kind of thing happened regularly. What would a towing company have to do with anything?

It was time to investigate a little more about the victim. There had to be a connection of some kind.

First, don't go off half-cocked. Maybe the truck they drove got hauled off or broke down or something such. There had to be a connection with Pablo, whatever it was. What?

Pablo was in Hornitos. He went to Chiriqui Grande regularly. He ... had a girlfriend in Chiriqui Grande. Was the connection because of that?

He drove to Hornitos. Pablo's girlfriend was Consuela Garcia Smith. Call her Connie. She was a pretty waitress in the Estrellas Sueños Restaurante, by the docks.

On to Chiriqui Grande. He found Connie, who said she didn't know what was wrong with Pablo for a couple of weeks before he died. He said there were crooks everywhere, and that he knew where something was that could tie the lot of them tightly together – in jail! There were Panamanians and Colombians and Israelis and even a Russian! One of them lived right there in Hornitos!

That jolted Clint. He remembered something that had flashed across his mind back at that fire scene. This was going to get too complicated if it went on much longer!

He headed for Hornitos, where he went directly to the police check stop and asked about Tonio, who was in David, at the time. He said he had to get some critical information, they said they had instructions to cooperate in any way.

"There's a company, a gruas, who had some kind of connection with a man, Vallartes, and Pablo and one other here."

"Gruas? They all come through here. We note the vehicles they pass ... Pablo. He and Santos worked with the gruas when they were needed in the mountains. They are experts for getting cars and trucks that have gone off the road and fallen. Let me check the ... (he went to a file cabinet and took out a file from about four months before) ... because someone from ... Vallartes. Mitsubishi truck. Broken axle. Gruas ... Superior. Pablo and Santos were on the truck ... because it picked up Vallartes' vehicle on the return from pulling that kerosene truck from Pelitas Angelas. Reason for request, some small tools were missing from the Vallartes vehicle when it reached David. Hmm. Came back next day and said the tools were in a box that was taken out and stored at ... Santos' place? ... Why would ... that's odd. They had it, and it was all a misunderstanding. The box was like the one Santos had and the ... Pablo thought it was his, and unloaded it at Santos place. He called the gruas, but they apparently forgot to call Vallartes."

"Got caught, huh?" Clint asked.

"Yes. The way it was done ... then Pablo is killed, and Santos has gone to visit his sister in Las Tablas?

"I wonder! What was in that box?"

"Something to kill for," Clint said dryly.

Back to David or ...?

Santos went into that house before the fire was entirely out and found the body. Clint didn't believe for a second that he killed Pablo. He was too scared. That meant something was in the house that Santos had to find. He wouldn't have gone in that soon, otherwise.

Clint went to the burned house and spent more than an hour rummaging. The locals had taken anything useful, and there was nothing but ashes and twisted metal inside. The bedsprings were still where they had been. Pablo's body was removed, and nothing else disturbed. There was probably nothing there Clint didn't see when he was there. He didn't miss much.

Unless it was under the body?

He found some old hardware cloth and started sifting the ashes under the springs. He found four large lumps of melted gold and two blackened platinum settings for necklaces. The settings were for large stones.

He sifted a bit more and fond two very large emeralds, one ruby, and two diamonds. He found a little steel card file box, but the paper inside was now nothing but dry powder ashes. That was probably a very important part of this.

He took out his cell phone and called Tonio. He explained what he had found, and suggested the ashes in that room be very carefully strained. There were at least four more smaller stones somewhere in that mess.

He waited ten minutes until Estevez, a cop from the check station, came to the house. He listed what he had found and where. Two men were coming from David to finish the job.

Clint used his digital camera and took closeups of the stones and settings he had, then gave them to Estevez. He had an idea those things were going to help solve this thing.

"Why did you even look here?" Estevez asked. "We thought we had done a thorough job."

"Because the old cliche about hiding the jewels and money under the mattress is true, sometimes."

Estevez nodded and grimaced. Clint took his picture and headed to the internet. He e-mailed the pictures to Manolo. Then he went to the hotel, cleaned up, went for a very late dinner, and went to bed. It had been a very long day. Tomorrow would probably be as long.

The morning was beautiful. Clint spent a bit of time on the net. He looked up Carl Griesbaum and found he had been famous for handcarved music boxes. He made the automatons, each unique, using a mechanism made in Germany that moved the head and whistled a tune. Dave's had a number inside in pencil. 077 or 097. It was a man carrying a lantern and a key, with a bottle in the coat pocket. Dave said it was a town crier. Everything was original.

There was a short thing on the news about some Indios in Chiriqui joining with some from Bocas del Toro in a protest against the government taking their land, which is unconstitutional. Clint had heard about the promises made when the Ojos de Aguas hydroelectric project was started that had not been done the way promised. Now, a *very* large discovery of copper that was planned to be mined in a strip mine fashion on the comarca. It would poison and destroy the ecology of a very large area. Clint sided a hundred percent with the Indios. It was their land, and now they were being treated the same way the US treated the Indians there. The difference here was that the Indio land was some of the best in Panamá. Now the government was going in and taking the land because of the money the copper would bring while mining it would destroy ten times as much as could be gained?

Politics as usual. Noriega was supposedly in Chiriqui, in a private hospital. Clint wondered if Martinelli would become another like Noriega if given the chance.

Save that crap for later. Now to find something to tie this mess around some cheap hoods' necks. Should he go to Hornitos, Chiriqui Grande? Bocas?

Several truckloads of soldiers went by, heading for the carretera. Surely Martinelli knew better than to use such crude tactics! International sentiment would turn against him! It would result in armed soldiers facing Indios who had nothing but some rocks and machetes. Sooner or later, someone would get killed!

Clint called a friend in Florida who followed the news. He hadn't heard anything about it.

This was getting scary! Here we go again! They would never learn. The internet would make it impossible to hide. How could anyone in politics here think this kind of thing had a chance of working? It was going to get messy. It would be a lot easier to freeze all action on the projects until meeting with the leaders of both sides could find a compromise.

Bocas. He was a Ngobe, by declaration. He would be with his friends and the people he considered family. He was getting his things together in the car when the TV said the roads in Bocas and Chiriqui were closed. Nothing was getting through. The commentator was trying to make it sound like the Indios were threatening the whole country. Interviews with people concerned, except a few government officials, were backing the Indios more than 90%.

Well, what could he do about his case here, in these conditions? The gruas was here in David, so that would be an avenue to explore. He found the company and checked around with a lot of the locals. It seemed that the place didn't have a good reputation. It was tied in with a junkyard and auto repair company who were known as cheap crooks and wannabe gangsters. They were mostly into property theft through bribing corrupt officials. Everyone knew what they were doing, but the courts and police refused to act.

Why is there always a bug in the beer? Clint loved Panamá and the people. These few could ruin investment with their schemes. They had already caused some very big companies to back off from coming to Panamá. Maybe Clint could see that these, at least, were out of business!

Chapter four

There were a few people in the Cantina Parque. This is a little local bar across from the entrance to Romero's Super Market. The talk was about the "insurrection." Most agreed that the Indios had been no more than second rate citizens for a long time in Panamá, and it was high time they were treated like people. Panamanians were mostly very strong on individual rights.

Clint managed to mention Perez. Only one man there, a minor official with IDAAN, had heard of him. "He's supposed to be a businessman who deals in old things and jewels and that kind of thing. Not much is known about him. except that there are some here that are very suspicious of a Colombian who would come to David and Bocas looking for those things. What there is will be in Panamá City. No one in the old families here in Chiriqui would ever sell the family memories. I don't think he's honest in all things.

"He got drunk and used some kind of tae-kwan-do at Brothers once. He almost killed a man. A lot of places on the carretera won't let him drink more than a beer. Those two he hangs around with are as bad. They're all usually nice enough, but none of them can hold his liquor. I hear they get that drunk about once in two months at that place they rent. The dueño signed a five year lease and can't make them move.

"This is what I heard. I'm not saying it's true, but I did once see a fight at that place when I was checking a hook-up. They didn't use any of that martial arts stuff, but they ran the Arauz brothers away. The Arauz brothers were supposed to be mean and dangerous, but it didn't take long for them to be hurt enough that they never went back yet. The Colombians are a lot rougher than most people, even if they don't act like it most of the time, or look like it.

"Didn't I see you at Ya Rock one night? You were with that nutty gringo who played the guitar and sang a lot of gringo things that most people thought was good, even though they don't often listen to music in English – well, most of them know words in English to a lot of the old rock music."

"Dave? He can be a real trip, sometimes," Clint replied. The subject was changed. He had what he wanted. Don't push. He finished his Balboa and left.

Next stop: Rey. He went in to talk with people he knew and be introduced to more. Some lived in the near area, but he learned nothing new about the Colombians, though the things he'd heard at the Cantina were more or less confirmed. Most of the time they were alright, but about every two months they got crazy for a day or two. They didn't actually start things, but they would more or less instigate. They liked to show people how tough they were.

"How long until they want to try it again?" he asked a three-houses-down neighbor.

"They're due."

Clint grinned. Maybe he'd be the next one they wanted to intimidate. He was fifty eight years old and in prime condition. They would think he was just a hotshot gringo easy pushover. They got started in two local bars, Chaco's and Music Night. They started there, but there was never any trouble inside the place was the only reason they were allowed.

Clint would be ready to barhop tonight! This was silly, but the only way he would be able to get them into a position where they would make a serious enough mistake that could lead to a deep official investigation. Clint knew a way to tie them to Pablo's death. It was murder. There had to be motive established. He could do that.

Clint dressed in old jeans and a "muscle" shirt

and wore Crocks. His beard was a three-day one already. He sported a tiger tatoo on one arm and a death head on the other. The tatoos wouldn't come off with regular soap and water or alcohol. They needed a special acetone-based paste solvent. His black-shot-with-gray hair was shoulder length and ponytail style. His belt was studded, and he wore a studded leather bracelet. He had one flashy ruby ring and a cheap rhinestone friendship ring. He had a small earring in his left ear. Diamond. He used the Hofai motorcycle a friend kept at Dave's place in Quiteño that was much like his own in Bocas Town. He had a large black leather wallet in his right back pocket, attached to his belt with a chain. He also wore an attitude of an old hippie biker.

He decided to start with Music Night because there was a live band of sorts there that was doing semi-rock in Spanish. They weren't bad, but they definitely weren't good. The talk was about the Indigeno uprising and was negative toward them. Almost half of the people there were blacks, who don't get along with the Indios.

Not much was happening there, so he went to Chaco's. Not much there, either, except that the Mitsubishi truck went by, going toward Music Night. That gave Clint an idea. Dave was in town, so he called and asked for a favor. Dave would come into Music Night in about an hour with his guitar. He would look a bit more hippie than usual.

Clint knew that Dave loved the Indios as much as he did. He could picture him in that crowd. He warned him it could be dangerous. Dave laughed and said that wouldn't be anything new. Everyone told him that going into the mountains and into the comarcas was dangerous, and he was safer there than in the middle of David!

Clint went into the bar and stood next to Pancho Vallartes at the bar. He was able to get him into a conversation, and was chatting about different things when Dave walked in and went to the other end of the bar to lean his guitar against the wall and order a large Atlas. Clint looked at him and said he thought he'd seen him in town, at Cervantes Park. He was playing for some Indios and talking with them about their situation.

"Martinelli should order the police to shoot every single one of them who start that bullshit!" he declared. "You can't let that bunch of pagan savages get control of the situation!"

"Didn't you say you were Colombian?" Clint asked.

"Yes. Santa Marta."

"Then why don't you keep your obnoxious

fucking bigoted opinions to yourself here in Panamá?"

"Yeah? What's it to you, gringo? *You* aren't Panamanian anymore than I am!"

"I'm Ngobe, so I'm Panamanian," Clint snarled. "You're an ignorant arrogant asshole shithead from Colombia!"

Pancho stared at him a few seconds, hissed, "Watch your back!" and started moving away. Clint called, "My back. You seem that type. I say what I have to say and do what I have to do in your face, fuckoff!"

Pancho stalked over to Perez and Simon and started a whispered conversation that included waving his arms and pointing at Clint, who gave them the bird. Clint went over to Dave, and said, "You were playing in Centro. You're not too bad. A hell of a lot better than that wad on the stage." Loud enough for the one nearest on the stage to hear.

"I played a few odd things from the sixties and early seventies for the Indios. We were protesting civil rights, back then, though we were working with the blacks – who seem to be the worst bigots here."

The band were one Latino and three blacks. The one who heard the exchange went to the others and said something. Their lead singer, such as he was, took the mike and announced they had a celebrity from the seventies in the states there. How about if he came up and did a few protest songs for his Indio friends. See how it went over in that *PANAMANIAN* place.

"The Indios are the only real Panamanians," Dave replied quietly. "*We* are the interlopers." He picked up his guitar and went to the stage and did *Come Together* and *Travelin' Man*. He was good at that kind of thing, and the crowd liked the songs. Pancho yelled that he should do something for the Indio friend he was talking to, seeing that seemed to be timely.

"Oh, yes. You're that fellow who was declared a Ngobe?" Dave asked. "I think this one should be taught to the Indios. Maybe I'll write something along the lines. I'll do it in Guayme."

He did *Blowin' In the Wind*, which the crowd really liked.

Clint stayed until Dave left, after doing two more numbers. Everyone liked his music, if not his views. Pancho, in particular, was steaming. As Dave went out, he was headed for the door. Clint stepped in front of him and said, "Go sit down, Colombian! Keep you fucking nose out of our affairs, here!" Four people close heard it, and said that seemed a good idea to them, too. They wouldn't go to Colombia and interfere with their politics. Have the decency to return the favor.

Pancho went back to his brother and Perez. Nobody would talk to them anymore.

The Panamanians here had different points of view than the Indios, but they deeply believed in compromise. They understood that the Indios had tried that, and it hadn't worked. They didn't like what was happening, but understood it. They wanted the government to back down before it got more violent.

The band left the stage and the bartender turned on the TV. The news was on. An Indio had been killed. A 26 year old man.

"Oh, *shit*!" the bartender cried. "Now it starts! Oh, SHIT!"

That fit Clint's reaction perfectly. The crowd was suddenly almost totally in sympathy with the Indios. They were afraid that this would make a compromise impossible.

"I think the Indio leaders will call for calm," Clint said. "There will be a strong reaction, but maybe the government will see that the whole world's watching and come to some kind of agreement while there's still a chance."

An Indio woman came on and called for her people to remain calm. Martinelli and the police would answer for that atrocity. The time for accord was fast coming to an end. Let there be no more violence.

Clint nodded. The bartender said he was now solidly for the Indios. There was no excuse for killing anyone. The whole world would get the idea Panamanians were a bunch of uncivilized barbarians. Noriega-types were again in charge! Clint agreed, but said Martinelli was a businessman who understood what that kind of thing would do. He would surely try to stop it. He was money-oriented, and this could hurt investment and tourism very badly.

He went back to the hotel. He expected the Colombians to lay for him, but they hadn't. Maybe they saw they could only lose to carry anything any further than they already had.

Chapter five

Tonight the Colombians would make some kind of move. The situation with the Indios had gotten worse, for a time, ending when the Indios burned the police station in Volcan. There were suddenly several meetings with the Indigeno's representatives, and an effort was being made to find some kind of meeting ground from which to work. The police had broken up the barricades on the roads, but it was still chancy to drive anywhere. Gasolene and foods were now coming into David. Another Indio, very young, was killed in Las Lomas. It was now critical that an agreement be reached, or there could be repercussions that would make it a concern past the borders of the country.

Clint would stay in the hippie/biker disguise tonight. He would go to places a little distanced from Chaco's and Music Night. The Colombians seemed to start at those two places and act in others a little farther away. If he could get them to attack him he could call in Tonio, say he was investigating Pablo's murder, this Perez character was in Hornitos and was interested in where

Pablo lived, he found the stolen items in Pablo's burned house, he was attacked here, those three always hang around together, they had gone to Chiriqui Grande, where Pablo's girlfriend said there was some kind of trouble between Pablo and those three, they represented an antique and jewelry dealer in Colombia, there were no antiques or jewels in Hornitos or Chiriqui Grande except the ones found in Pablo's house. There is some kind of money laundering scheme being run by the person they met in Chiriqui Grande. Two and two are still four.

Tonio would greatly enjoy hearing that list of "clues" Clint had discovered. and would insist on a complete investigation of all those named and concerned. When they had given their statements, he would throw in his ace.

Clint was at Rey just before six o'clock, had a comida corriente in a local restaurant he would definitely remember. It was good! Two dollars, and all he could eat. He had a choice of pollo, loma, mondongo, carne, puerco. or pescado. He took the carne with aroz, frijoles, and a salad.

He was waiting to see the Mitsubishi drive by about seven when he got a call from Samuel, a police officer he knew. Dave was attacked by two men. He wasn't harmed, and had used a pepper spray on them and had knocked one of them down and kicked him in the face before a third shoved him aside and pushed the two into a red truck. No one was close enough to identify anyone, but Dave told him they were Colombians he had seen last night when he played some music in a bar over near Rey.

Clint started to get royally pissed, then thought about it. Seventy five year old Dave, five eight and a hundred forty pounds, taking on three Colombians half his age and twice his size. It was almost funny.

He called Dave, who said it was no big deal. He figured that was about what Clint wanted. and had carried pepper spray for that reason. He hadn't counted on the third one being able to get them away, but maybe Clint didn't need that.

"It's just an item to add to a list, but don't get involved with my shit to where you get hurt."

"I suppose they'll try something a little worse soon, but I have to go to Punta Piedra tonight, so won't be here. Too bad!"

"I want them to come after me. It'll be the lever I need to find out what's really going on with that woman and her gringo boyfriend in Chiriqui Grande."

"Linda? That restaurant bit?"

"Uh-huh."

"It's a tired old scheme to launder money. They're Colombians. DUH!"

"It's not drugs."

There was a short pause. Dave asked, "Is that certain?"

"Directly, yes. It could still be something that was originally financed through drugs, but they're not there anymore."

"Know what it is?"

"Not even a good suspi.... I might have an idea, but Santa Marta? Why Santa Marta?"

"What?"

"It's not in that area."

"Which makes good old Santa Marta a great place to run it, maybe?"

"Could be. It just could be!"

"Watch your back!"

"Yeah. You too. One of them suggested the same thing, but in a different tone."

They chatted a little, then Clint rung off and sat back to think, over another cup of coffee. "Why Santa Marta?" could be the same question as "Why Chiriqui Grande?"

Should he change tactics?

If they came by within the next hour, keep to the plan. If not ... maybe wait another day or two. He thought a bit more, then called Manolo. "Is there a big trade in stolen jewelry in Santa Marta,

Colombia?”

“Not that we know of.”

“I think just maybe now you know of.”

“Tonio sent me descriptions and pictures of what you found in Hornitos. The one emerald is large enough to be of interest to us, but there’s no indication it’s anything illegal. It’s not reported missing anywhere, and it’s worth about a mil and a half.”

“Manolo, I think there’s a big find somewhere in northern Colombia. Emeralds. I think they’re on government land or something. I think you can find out what’s going on. Trace the Colombians I asked about from the first time they farted to the last.”

“Will do! You might have found something. Some trades in unregistered large stones have been showing up in Sweden. They might have come through Australia. No one can prove anything. We have to treat them as legitimate, even though we damned well know better.”

They chatted until the Mitsubishi went by. Clint decided to wait until he had more information.

The truck stopped and backed up. Clint sighed. It wouldn’t hurt anything.

Donaldo got out and came to where he was sitting. “I’m not looking for trouble. We were out of line. I just want to know what Clint Faraday finds so interesting about us.

"You see, that old hippie said that about you being the one who was declared a Ngobe. We checked."

"Maybe it wasn't you I was interested in – until last night."

"May I ask who, then?"

"You can ask, but I won't answer. It was to do with some things that happened in two places, neither in David. It's tied into a murder."

"But ... you confronted my brother last night. I don't know why?"

"We were just chatting like people do in a bar when he made a snide remark about killing off the Indios. I am a Ngobe. He was suddenly not the sort of okay guy I was talking to in a bar, he was a bigoted piece of shit who wasn't even from this country."

"That's all it was?"

"Then. I'll probably let it drop if nothing else happens. If something else happens I won't let it go."

"Nothing will happen to you. I've already said we've decided it was our own doing."

"To me or my friends, you have a deal." Clint offered his hand. Donaldo looked sick and shook it. Clint let it be a dead fish type of contact. That "...or my friends," hit him right in the gut. Hard.

It was as good as a physical blow. It was already done – but the fact Dave came out on top and wasn't hurt might be passed, if they were lucky.

They weren't lucky. That was why he stated it like that.

It did call for a slight change of plans. He had to keep it tied or too much could be lost.

Chapter six

"Mr Hanrady? You left your number. I'm Lila Green? At the antique shop?"

Clint stared at the phone a second. He hadn't left his number. "Yes?"

"I have a solid offer for the Griesbaum, but you didn't return. I hope you haven't sold it?"

"Er, no. I was tied up with another matter. I still want to move it for my friend. He needs the money for a legal matter.

"I thought ... I didn't remember to give you my number. I thought of that after I'd left, but I'd said I'd be back, and didn't think more about it."

"You gave me the description paper. It has your number on it. 'Call for information' is on the bottom."

"Oh! Right! I forgot!"

"Well, I have very good news! My friend in Colombia will pay three five, which is a little better than I thought!" she cried. "Mr. Hanrady, he is a lot more interested than he first seemed. I think, if your friend is willing to wait, he can get even more than five thousand, in a few days!

"I usually wouldn't tell a client that, but my

commission is a percent, so I want it as high as possible. There was some kind of thing on the net, E-Bay or something, where a Griesbaum in very good condition went for more than twelve thousand dollars! A description pointed out that these are hand-carved by a great artist who has been dead some years now, so there will never be more. They could appreciate at fantastic rates if Southerby's and such took a special interest."

"I'll ask my friend if he wants to wait. I'll call back in a few minutes," Clint promised. "I have the number on caller ID."

"Please do!"

Clint called Dave, who said to get what he could. There really wasn't any hurry, because his case probably wouldn't get to court for weeks. This is, after all, Panamá!

Clint called back and said they could wait a week or so to see what happened. She seemed happy about that. Clint went to the internet to check. It seemed the Griesbaum was on a site that specialized in such things, and that the sale actually happened. He knew Griesbaum would appreciate at a steady rate. This was too much. What was going on?

He called Manolo. Manolo would call back in ten minutes.

In ten minutes: "From Santa Marta, Colombia.

What's going on?"

"I think I see what's happening here. They're getting too much money to launder in the regular ways, and things might get hot pretty fast. Suppose you had millions to move, with ways that could only move hundreds of thousands? What could you do to legitimize that much?

"Look! A Carl Griesbaum automaton is on sale at a website. I checked. It's been there for months with bids of two thousand, which was under the minimum bid of two two fifty. There's an offer in a little town in Panamá to purchase one.

"You bid a very high price for the one on the net. The value of all Griesbaum collectibles skyrockets. You might pay, say, ten thousand for the one in Panamá, making *two* huge sales to buttress the one on the net. Suddenly you're getting bids in the millions for the things, if they're in excellent to perfect condition. You offer your two through Southerby's and put a shill or two in the bidders. Suddenly you have a way to move millions."

"But ... it damned well could work if you get two opposing European markets into it. I wish I had a couple more of those things stored in the attic! I could be a millionaire in a couple of months!"

"Now to stop this crap!"

"Wait until *after* Dave sells his. Make him hold out for twenty five grand, minimum. If this is the scheme, they'll go for it. The more they have to pay for his, the higher the bidding goes in a week in the international marketplace. They'll *want* him to raise the price!"

"And the simple fact that such prices were paid for Griesbaum's establishes their base price, whether this bunch is in it or not," Clint replied, with a laugh. "This is getting to be fun! Everyone else is manipulating the markets in a lot of ways to make a dishonest buck or two. Why not us?"

"Our end isn't dishonest," Manolo pointed out.

"There is that bit!" Clint rang off and giggled. Dave would get a real kick out of this.

He called Lila and said his friend knew about the sale on the net and said that would establish a market that could well go into the hundreds of thousands in a couple of months. He would sell, but he would want a third of what the value would be if this caught on. Thirty grand, or he'd wait.

They had to establish the market, and wanted it high. She said five minutes for her to dicker with her bidder. Clint waited. She called back and said she had made a great deal for all of them! Her buyer had figured the same way, and would give his friend a third of what his projection indicated.

Thirty seven five! Cash! He would pay the fees and commissions!

Clint said he'd bring the automaton in as soon as she could get the cash. She said within the hour. There was a direct transfer account with that bidder. He would have the cash money there instantly.

Clint said he'd be right over.

He got his disguise on as quickly as he could, and took the Griesbaum to the shop. This had to be legitimate from this end. It would surely be checked, so he knew she had arranged that. He suggested the money should be directly transferred to Dave's account. She said she had the cash, that she'd already gone to the bank just across at Rey and gotten the cash money. She got her own commission immediately, that way. It had actually saved her business, because she hadn't sold anything much in more than a week, and was afraid she wouldn't make the rent. Now she could pay for a year in advance and sleep at night without worry!

Clint made out a receipt. She locked the automaton in her safe and they went to the notary office for the receipt to be officially registered. It made the entire process in Panamá legitimate. Clint went to HSBC with his copy and the cash and deposited it in Dave's account. When Clint saw the account on the computer screen there, he shook his head. Dave had two dollars and thirty six cents in the bank before the deposit was made. Clint knew this would be gone in no time. Dave spent all he had helping people. He was like that.

He called Manolo. "Well?"

"Not a penny transferred from anywhere. She had the cash right there in her office she couldn't pay the rent for. Did you get a look in that safe when she put the thing in?"

"No. She made damned sure I couldn't see."

"I wonder what else is in that safe."

"You and me, both."

"Well, now we can set something up where they'll get caught with a lot of unexplainable cash or with as much or more in jewels. If it's a large find, they'll be uncut. Try to explain that!"

They chatted a few minutes, and Clint rang off. He went to his hotel and got rid of the disguise. He went to Las Brasas for a good rib-eye, then to the 7 Mares to chat with Ulyses and Alan, then to Sandy's for a few minutes. He decided to go to Cantina Parque for one beer, then to the Iris for the last one at Peter's. Perez was at the Cantina Parque, but he only nodded at Clint and left soon.

Clint wanted to solve the murder. He had an idea that could put both him and Manolo in a good position to close their parts out. He hoped to have it done before Carnaval, just three more days. He hoped he could get to Las Tablas. The pageant there was a lot like Mardi Gras in New Orleans!

Martinelli had just announced he wouldn't negotiate with the indigenos until after Carnaval holidays? That pretty much told Clint how much he actually cared about the people in Panamá! He had started out thinking Martinelli would become a truly great president, but he was apparently another like the bunch before him. Another politician on the make. That might make for trouble over the holidays that would definitely get international attention! All negative!

Well, Dave's experiences had shown the system to be as corrupt as it always was. It would take another hundred plus years to stop or change it if all the politicians did was talk. They were the source of it. That's why they're politicians. Clint thought he could handle things by manipulation within the law. He didn't need and wouldn't use the corruption. He knew how to get around a lot of it.

He'd have to, actually. This bunch would have the money to offer some very high bribes. The one thing that bunch fear is anyone getting proof of what they are and going public. He already had a couple of things that certain underlings couldn't hope to explain, which meant they would have to bring their superiors into it.

Did he want to get involved in that?

Why the hell not?

<u>*Chapter seven*</u>

The trick was going to be in getting them to collect a lot of money together. A good lever was their dealing in jewels. It was widely known that he was involved with finding two multi-million dollar treasure finds. They would have to get their hands on a certain amount of legitimate, so far as could be shown, material. He could use the reputation of corruption in his favor. there. He had the contact established. Lila Honey was about to get a hint about a cache of jewels that were, in a word, unreported. They could be legitimized easily for a few lousy thousand dollars in the right place. The main thing this bunch had to avoid was having their find located.

He called Dave, who pointed out that he would be suspected because of the thing with the bar. Why not use Judi? She was more than capable!

He called Judi, who agreed to send an e-mail to Hanrady and another tomorrow. He went to the internet and set up a free e-mail account with Mail.com. He spent an hour setting up a bunch of e-mails for the registry, both ways, made a phone call, and put on the Hanrady disguise. He called

Lila when he received the second one and said he had something she might be interested in. They could all three make a lot on it. She had already made a small hint that she knew someone who could handle what he had.

"I did?"

"You said the Griesbaum was probably found in an attic somewhere, or something such. You don't have to be a genius to know what that meant!"

She laughed. "What do you have?"

"I'll come over there. You have a computer on the net?"

"Computer? Well, yes?"

"I want you to read an e-mail I just got. I said we would all *three* make a lot."

"Half an hour?"

"I'll be there."

He called Manolo and told him what was going down. This could keep everyone's name out of it on the legal end.

He caught a cab and was at Lila's just fifteen minutes late, which was early in Panamá.

She greeted him and said she hoped it was something as good as the Griesbaum. He laughed and said that was a little diversion, nothing more. He did that for a friend. This one, he wanted a hunk of.

"I'll just let you read the e-mail, then we can contact the one who ... you'll see."

She led him into the little office and waved at the computer. He sat down and brought up his e-mail, answered two "new" ones and erased the half-dozen scams and penis enlargement offers. He shook his head.

"Yeah. It used to be Cialis and Viagra, now it's that crap. You guys seem to have a lot of trouble with certain physical features."

"And you women get as many boob enlargement kinds of things. Here it is."

She sat at the desk and read the e-mail. He noticed she had seen the long lists of e-mails, so would think the site had been used for some time.

Snra. Lum – I realize you won't know who I am. We met twice before in casual encounters, once at the garden club dinner and once at The Reef Restaurante. The meeting at The Reef is why I am contacting you. You were talking about your friend who had found the two pirate treasure chests on Solarte. You said it was a shame the government would get all the money because the people here need it a lot more than a bunch of cheap snakes in government.

*I have found something that might have been part of that, though the police believe all was found. It is a smaller chest, but contains **kilos** of* *jewels and gold. I would like to propose a business deal under which the government would not get everything. I feel they got enough already and your penchant for financing many hospitals and schools for the Indigenous people is known everywhere.*

I am an Indigeno myself. I could, because of that fact, not hope to get away with disposing of what must be a million dollars or more in jewels. I think that you will know some way to handle this so that my people will get the main part of the money. I will meet you if you will call me. I know that, even if you will not do this, you will also not turn me in to the police. I will call you at exactly two o'clock on catorce de Febrero. Juan Pablo (not my name)

"That was the first one, last night. It was, as you can see, a forwarded message from Mrs. Lum, a friend in Bocas. I got the next one two hours ago. At three twenty, as the time will tell you on the message. I considered it and decided to call you. Here were are."

He brought up another message seven down the list.

Jim – I just looked at what the man I will call Juan Pablo has. He is an Indio I know well, and I know his impossible situation.

I would usually refuse to even listen, but it is

"She knows this kind of stuff better than anyone else in Panamá. What can you arrange?"

"I know someone who has a good in with the government. He can work an authentication deal, for a price. I know about those treasures that gringo found. A business acquaintance of mine helped some people, shall we say, dispose of part of it?"

"What kind of deal? No screwing the Indios. Judi wouldn't go along with that, and neither would I."

"They can't expect or get market prices, but I can see they get more ... this Judi character is a good appraiser?"

"The best."

"We have to forget the historical part. I think we can get the seven million and maybe just a little more. I'll have to make a call?"

"Tomorrow morning at eight. You have my number." He logged off the e-mail. He knew she'd save the two. He had excellent peripheral vision and had seemed to be looking away when she quickly saved them. He counted on that. They would check the source and time and find they were pretty much what Clint suggested. The source would be an internet café in Bocas.

He went back to his hotel and called Manolo to set things up. He had checked on the cash received form with the bank Lila had supposedly used to accept the "transfer" from Colombia and knew it was a phony she gave to Dave's bank. She would work the same type of deal here. Manolo could check that kind of thing with banks in minutes. This would happen fast, now.

He relaxed, had a good meal at La Tipica with Annette, a girl from France he met. He spent the night at her place. It was a great night!

At precisely eight o'clock in the morning he got

a call. "I'll have the cash here by nine thirty. It's being delivered as soon as the bank's machines can count it. Eight two. It'll be in hundreds."

"I'll have ... why can't we just make a standard bank transfer?"

"Because we're working a little bit outside of normal business practices. We don't want to leave a direct trail to us or to the ones we're dealing with."

"I suppose that'll be a large crate. I don't know how much that much will take. It'll be heavy!"

"It's eight thousand two hundred hundreds. That's a hundred sixty stacks. That's a stack five feet deep. Packed in a box three stacks long by five wide make a box eight inches deep. It'll weigh about eighteen pounds."

"Sheesh! The jewels take up more space!"

"Yes. Money's a more efficient way to store the value. It's not nearly so stable."

"You got that! I'll be there!"

He called Manolo. It would go down before ten o'clock.

He ate a good breakfast of hojaldres and boletas and met Manolo, who "wired" him with a little recorder that wasn't much larger than a cigarette lighter and looked like one. It broadcast through his phone.

Clint went into the gift shop with an Indio

friend, Emilio, who would play the innocent idiot to perfection. It was an act he used on the snobbery gringos. He spoke very good English, but would act like all he understood was "Bullshit!" and "Money!" and "Ello, my friend!" He was carrying a heavy box that Manolo had filled with very fancy antique jewelry. It was mostly very good copies, but was put together by experts. It would take another expert to say it wasn't authentic.

Lila looked through it and lifted some of the gold, part of which was real gold. "Heavy!" she said.

"Gold is," he replied. She looked at the large emeralds and rubies and almost drooled. They were good!

"Well, you kept your end. I'll get the cash."

She went around the corner and opened the safe to take out a box. She turned back to find Manolo and two agents standing there with automatic weapons pointed at Clint and Emilio. They were looking shocked and scared.

"I'll take that, Mrs. Green. I am Manolo, an agent for Interpol. We've been watching you for a time, since jewels we traced to here showed up in Australia. We detained your three Colombian friends in the alley in back. I'm afraid it'll be some years before any of your little group will be allowed to leave Panamá to spend whatever part you've been able to hide so far."

She fainted. Manolo shook his head sadly and shrugged at Clint.

"Oh! I meant to tell you. We took a picture of Perez to Hornitos. He's been identified as the one who was there before Pablo was murdered. We're also watching the gringo in Chiriqui Grande and his lovely girlfriend. It seems he came here after midnight last night for some odd reason. I think maybe his prints are going to be all over that box, don't you?"

"I won't be surprised," Clint agreed.

They went to the station, where Clint and Emilio made their statements. Judi would give hers in a notarized declaration. Perez and the Vallarte brothers had some hard explaining to do. Perez was going down for the murder of Pablo. Santos would come back from Las Tablas to testify with immunity for stealing the jewels in the first place. All-in-all, not a bad resolution!

Clint sat back in the seat. They were on their way to Las Tablas. Judi was driving. They had just been passed through a blockade by the Indios at Mali. They got a lot of really hard dirty looks from the people backed up. Clint had gone off the main road just before Mali and through a pasture that belonged to a friend. He had come out on the electric station road, where he was past the main part of the blockade. The people here knew him and greeted him warmly. He told them to stick to their guns, but to be careful. Things could get very bad. They went on through and didn't have anymore trouble. The police at the check point at La Mina couldn't believe they'd gotten through. He said he had friends.

They went on through Gualaca and to the main carretera, then into David. They didn't have anymore trouble until they were outside of Tolé. They didn't know many of the Indigenos here, but they knew who Clint was and showed him a way through the comarca to the highway past. The next stop was Santiago, where they didn't have any trouble. They ate a good meal at The

Pyramid, talked with people they knew, then proceeded to Las Tablas, where you would think it was the main carnaval parade in progress – which would be tomorrow noon. They would stay at a gringo friend's place for the night. It was a non-stop party time. It was very much like Mardi Gras in New Orleans, in some ways. Tomorrow was the really big day. The twenty first.

"I think there's a fire dead ahead," Judi said. "Should we stop?"

"No."

C. D. Moulton's works are available on most major outlets as printed or e-books. CD writes the CD Grimes, PI mysteries, the Det. Lt. Nick Storie mysteries, the Clint Faraday mysteries, the Flight of the Maita science fiction series, books on orchid culture and many others of many types. Mystery, adventure, intrigue, science fiction, fantasy, para-normal, mild erotica, and factual.